TOM **PALMER**

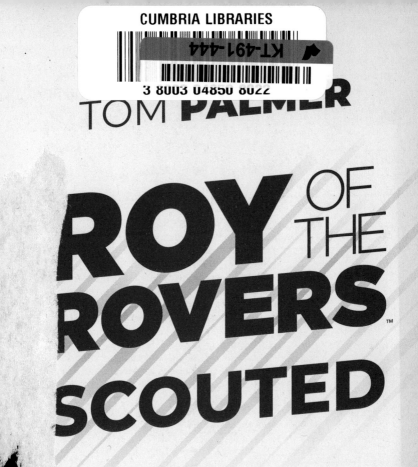

ROY OF THE ROVERS™

SCOUTED

Illustrated by
Lisa Henke

REBELLION®

First published 2018 by Rebellion Publishing Ltd,
Riverside House, Osney Mead,
Oxford, OX2 0ES, UK

www.rebellionpublishing.com

ISBN: 978 1 78108 698 8

10 9 8 7 6 5 4 3 2 1

A CIP catalogue record for this book is available
from the British Library.

Designed & typeset by Rebellion Publishing Ltd

Printed in Denmark

A Rebellion publication
www.royoftheroversofficial.com
info@royoftheroversofficial.com

Follow us:

royoftheroversofficial   royoftheroversofficial   royoftherove

Creative Director and CEO: Jason Kingsley
Chief Technical Officer: Chris Kinglsey
Editor: Rob Power   Design: Sam Gretton   Cover image: Ben Willshe

For Simon Robinson

Roy Race read in a magazine that to be really good at something you have to practice doing it 10,000 times.

Ten.

Thousand.

Times.

Inspired by what he'd read, Roy had dedicated his summer holidays to working on his footballing weakness, something he wanted to make into a footballing strength.

Volleying.

And now the moment had come for the practice to pay off.

Sunday morning in mid-September. Time for the first game of the season, which was always a big game. But, for Roy, it was an even bigger game. Today Roy was making his debut for the Grimroyd Under-18s.

The Moor had once been wild heather-smothered moorland above Melchester, Roy's home city. Now it was half a dozen waterlogged football pitches, where every autumn, the eight teams who used the pitches as their home ground played out a pre-season cup competition.

There was even a trophy. The Moor Cup.

Round one. Grimroyd v Low Moor.

Within minutes of kick off Roy realised that practicing alone in his back yard had been poor preparation for playing against the city's eighteen-year-olds. His coach – Yunis Khan – had told him to play up front, just behind the main striker. Coach wanted Roy to receive the ball, back to goal, then play the midfielders in as they surged forward.

That was the plan. On paper.

On the pitch it was different.

The first time Roy did what he was asked he felt a painful jab in his back and found himself on the floor. The second time, his defender went straight through him. Roy stood up, dusted himself down and looked up into the eyes of the six-foot-three giant who was marking him.

'You're out of your depth, sunshine,' the giant growled.

Roy smiled at the defender, noticing his arms were thicker than Roy's legs.

One chance, Roy said to himself. *I just need one chance to show you I'm not.*

Roy Race wasn't the only one being hammered that morning on the pitch. His friend, Lofty Peak, was being punished too. And there was reason for that: Lofty had been on the books of the city's Premier League team, Tynecaster United, since the age of six. But, at the end of last season, he'd been released. Lofty's history – and the fact that he was six-foot-five – made him a marked man, with everyone desperate to prove they were better than him. Which was why Lofty was on the grass writhing in agony after an elbow to the throat.

Half time arrived. Roy gazed out across the other council pitches. Rusty goal posts with ragged nets. An old man with his dog, watching the action. Roy knew him. The man was Fred. The dog, Rover. A regular on the Moor.

'This is tough,' Roy said, his attention back on Lofty.

His friend looked miserable. 'Get used to it,' he scowled. 'It's part of the game. They're bigger than you. They've got more muscle. They'll use it, however good a player you are.'

Roy and Lofty trudged to the side of the

pitch and slumped on the grass, waiting for Yunis to give his half-time talk.

'So that elbow in the neck was just part of the game?' Roy asked.

'It was,' Lofty said, gingerly touching his skin where a bruise was forming.

Suddenly a shadow blocked out the sun. But it wasn't a cloud. It was Vinny Sampson, the Grimroyd team captain. Vinny looked like he was in his late twenties, even though he was only eighteen. His eyes had something wild about them.

'Boys,' Vinny growled. 'You two might think you're all grown up now you're in my team, but you're playing like five-year-olds. Get it together, understand?'

Roy nodded.

Vinny walked off, shaking his head and muttering something about kids. Roy thought again about his defender and how he could prove the defender and Vinny wrong.

Yunis' team talk was short and clear, given with a mysterious grin on his face. They were playing well, he said. The game was tight. Games like this were decided by one goal and one mistake. Yunis urged the players keep positive – and not make that mistake.

Then he told them the reason he was smiling.

'I've had some great news,' he said. 'Great news for you. The kind of news that could change your life. I'll tell you more after the match, but do your best to win this, then the news could be even better.'

Roy took what Lofty had said on board in the second half. He got stuck in, ran hard at the defence, gave every pass, tackle and aerial challenge one hundred per cent. He was intrigued by what Yunis had said. What did he mean when he said news that could change their lives?

The only goal of the game was from a corner. Roy ran in from the edge of the area to try to connect to midfielder Dave Brayley's corner, but the menacing defender, who had been tracking him all game, guided Roy away from the ball with his shoulder. The ball skimmed off the defender's head but then, appearing as if from out of nowhere, Lofty was in on it, his forehead directing the ball through the keeper's flailing arms.

GOAL!

Grimroyd 1 – 0 Low Moor.

Roy smiled and caught the eye of his defender. The Low Moor giant looked angry and Roy didn't want to make him any angrier. But Roy knew he'd played a part in the goal – and that the defender knew that too. He'd pulled the defender out of position, caused him to make a rash header. And the goal came from that. It wasn't a volley, but that didn't matter to Roy.

When the referee blew for full-time, Roy tramped off the pitch and stood with the other players. The aftermath of the match felt strange to Roy. In the Under-16s team he had been the star player, the match winner, the player everyone mobbed at the end of the game to say well done. It was very different today. Roy didn't feel confident enough to look his teammates in the eye. He wasn't even sure he'd done enough even to justify keeping his place in the team. He'd been out-muscled and out-thought. He had a lot of learning to do.

But none of that seemed to bother Yunis. He was grinning from ear to ear.

'Gather round, lads,' Yunis said. 'Well done. Now listen. Here's the big news…'

Yunis gathered the Grimroyd Under-18 team into a circle.

'First of all, congratulations lads,' he said. 'We've made it to the last four of the Moor Cup. I know you must be tired and wanting to get away, but before you do, I've got news for you. I really think you're going to love this.'

'Love what?' Vinny grumbled, his bag already on his shoulder. 'Hurry up Yunis, I've got a snooker match to get to.'

'Bear with me for a minute, Vinny, will you?' Yunis rubbed his hands together. 'Now then. I've a question for you. Have any of you heard of Johnny Dexter?'

Roy put his hand up and immediately heard one or two of his new team mates laugh. He quickly realised why. He'd put his hand up. Like a schoolboy.

Roy didn't mind too much, though: he just wanted to explain who Johnny Dexter was.

'Yes, Roy,' Yunis said.

'Johnny Dexter is a legend! He played for Melchester Rovers as a defender and midfielder in the '90s. His nickname was "the Hard Man." He played eight times for England!'

'That's right, Roy,' Yunis confirmed. 'And Johnny Dexter is now coaching the Melchester Rovers youth team.'

Roy studied Coach. Why was Yunis talking about Johnny Dexter and Rovers' youth team?

'So, has he died or something?' Vinny asked.

Coach stared hard at Vinny, then quickly shook his head and turned to address the rest of team. 'No, Vinny. Johnny Dexter is still very much alive. In fact he's so alive that he's scouting all the local leagues looking for talent. He just texted me to say that Melchester Rovers needs a dozen local lads for an expanded youth squad. And he's coming to see us along with the twenty or so other local teams that...'

'When?' Roy interrupted.

'Soon.'

'But when?' Roy asked, hearing some of the other players laughing at him again. He knew they thought he was a little kid. But he didn't care. He needed to know the answer. He had always dreamed of being scouted by Melchester Rovers.

Yunis rubbed his chin. 'I don't know for sure, Roy, but it could be the semi on Wednesday, or it could be the final on Sunday, if we qualify for it. Just make sure you're here every game and every training session, all of you. Got it?'

'Rovers are rubbish,' Vinny sneered.

'League Two rubbish?' Yunis said harshly to his captain. 'Professional footballer rubbish? Really?'

Roy ignored Vinny and looked at the rest of the Grimroyd Under-18 players, and saw the hope in their eyes, some of them chatting excitedly because they'd just been told they had a shot at getting a trial at Melchester Rovers, for a professional football team.

'And, whether he's here or not, make sure we win the semi,' Yunis shouted, his team dispersing, before turning to Roy and extending an arm around his shoulder.

'Now, a word, young Mr Race.'
 Roy felt Yunis pull him gently away from
the others.

'Roy?'
'Yes, Coach.'
'You worked hard today.'

'Thanks, Coach.' Roy was waiting for a but.

'But,' Yunis went on, 'to be brutally honest, you looked a bit out of your depth.'

Roy nodded. He knew it.

'You need to work on strength,' Yunis said. 'You need to toughen up and wise up. The game is different at this level. Do you agree?'

'I do.'

'If the opposition push you,' Yunis went on, 'you have to push back – hard. If you don't they'll just ease you out of the way when you get near the penalty area. Like that defender did for that corner near the end of the second half. Are you with me, Roy?'

'Yes, Coach.'

'So when they come at you, go at them, put your shoulder in. Hard. If you can use your momentum to counter their momentum, you can stay on your feet and do what you want to do with the ball. Don't let them bully you. You have to be physical now you're playing bigger lads. Otherwise your talent counts for nothing. Watch how other players do it. Learn. Be clever.'

'Yes, Coach.'

'I know what you've got, Roy, because I've watched you playing for years and you are – without question – the most talented young footballer I have ever seen. But I always knew that moving up to this level would be your greatest challenge. You were an extraordinary player when you were a kid, but you're not playing against kids any more. Understand?'

'Yes, Coach.'

'And one more thing,' Yunis added. 'You need to be more vocal. Call for the ball and shout at your teammates to demand the ball from them, even off Vinny. Okay?'

'Yes, Coach.'

'I mean it, Roy, you have to demand it, claim it, insist they give the ball to you. Or they just won't.'

Roy said thank you to Yunis and, with all the other players from his game gone, he stayed on to watch the one remaining Under-18 game, one that had kicked off half an hour later than Grimroyd's.

He wanted to learn.

Fred and Rover came to join him.

'Roy.'

'Fred.'

'How's your dad?'

'Getting better,' Roy said, kneeling to stroke Rover, his eyes still on the football.

'Tell him I was asking after him.'

'I will.'

The old man coughed. 'I was watching

you. Playing, like.'

'Yeah?' Roy said.

'Yeah. You're going to have to work harder to match these lads,' Fred said.

Roy looked at the old man. 'I know,' he said. 'You're right. But I will.'

MONDAY MORNING. THE day after the game.

Roy's alarm went off at six. He jumped out of bed. Nobody else was about. His mum had gone out to work at half-five. His dad and sister, Rocky, were still in bed, giving Roy until seven o'clock before he had to get his dad up.

The weather looked mild and dry outside, so Roy threw on some shorts, an old hoody and his training shoes. The trainers were falling apart, the soles coming loose, but Roy had glued them again. Fully dressed, opening and closing the front door as quietly as he could, Roy collected his football from behind the bins, then jogged gently up the road, low brown terraced houses either side. He kept the ball at his feet, knocking it two or three metres ahead of him, warming his muscles and lungs. He passed cats on walls, men walking dogs, a woman driving a car away.

Once Roy reached the council football pitches, he ran around the Moor at medium pace, striking the ball harder now, left foot, then right.

One lap complete, Roy hit the grass at the very edge of the hillside. Time for strength work. He had researched what he had to work on. Legs. Arms. Core. He did twenty-five press ups, twenty-five sit ups, twenty-five burpees.

Then he did the whole set of exercises again.

Now Roy rested, staring out across the city, blood thundering round his body. He felt stronger. And that was the point. If he was going to cope in the Under-18s, he needed strength. Like Yunis had said.

The sun was up now, great shafts of light illuminating the football pitches and the city beyond them. Roy let his mind drift as he recovered for three minutes, gazing at the silvery thread of the river reflecting the sun as is flowed through the city.

The club's looking for a dozen local lads. For an expanded youth squad.

Those were Yunis' words.

But why? That's what Roy wanted to know. Why were Melchester Rovers expanding their youth squad when everyone knew the club hadn't enough money even for first team players? How could they afford to invest in players who might not play first team football for two or three years?

What was going on? And what could it mean for Roy?

The dream. That's what it could mean. Roy's dream of playing for Melchester Rovers.

Roy was on his feet, more motivated than ever. He'd done his strength, so now he needed to push his fitness, and not just his running-round-a-field fitness. He wanted to go harder than that. Roy jogged over to the edge of the Moor and stared down the Terrible 200. A double century of steps that led steeply from the Moor down to the bus station in the city. Everyone who lived around the Moor avoided the Terrible 200 if they could. They would rather take the fifteen-minute bus from the bus stop at the bottom than face the steps.

But not Roy Race.

Roy checked his watch, then, without hesitating, launched himself down the hill, his ball tucked under one arm, two steps at a time, watching every footfall in case he twisted or slipped. It was dangerous on the way down. He gone flying more than once on the Terrible 200. But today he stayed on his feet and made it to the bottom in seventy seconds.

Hearing the beep-beep of buses reversing,

he turned, without a rest, to head back up the Terrible 200.

Roy started steady. Taking the steps in twos, keeping his breathing even. Two thirds of the way up, Roy's whole body was hurting. But he knew that was good. If he was hurting, he was pushing his fitness.

What was it his dad used to say?

No pain, no gain.

Now every step was agony. Roy's brain saying stop, sit down, you've trained hard enough, just stop. But Roy didn't listen. He needed to go through the rest of the day knowing that he'd done the Terrible 200 properly.

He slowed as he neared the top. It was agony now; throat burning, legs jelly, Roy felt more like he was swimming up from the bottom of a lake with a concrete block tied to his feet.

One last push to get it up the last ten steps. He counted them out. Then, successful, Roy collapsed onto his hands and knees, retching, gasping in air.

He felt exhausted. But this was how he was going to make his dream come true. *No pain, no gain.*

Roy checked his watch, then turned to head back down the Terrible 200. He'd do it all a second time. Then he needed to get home. His dad would be waiting for him. He wanted to talk to his dad about the Melchester Rovers match that evening. Kelburn United at home. Roy couldn't wait.

Roy jogged home with the ball at his feet. He'd read on a sports fitness website that, right now, his legs would be filling with lactic acid from the hard training and that he needed to flush it out. A gentle run would achieve that, then his legs wouldn't hurt the next time he trained or played.

Back home, Roy showered, then, still feeling his post-exercise buzz, went into his parents' room to find his dad sitting up in bed listening to the sports news on the radio.

Dad's wheelchair was at the end of the bed where Roy had parked it the night before.

Danny Race winked his right eye at Roy. People used to say that father and son looked alike, but that wasn't the case anymore.

Roy was tall and lean with a flash of blond hair and a decent sun tan from spending the whole summer outside. His dad was pale and had lost a lot of weight. There was a long, stitched wound on the bald bit of his head that reminded Roy of a zip. Danny Race was

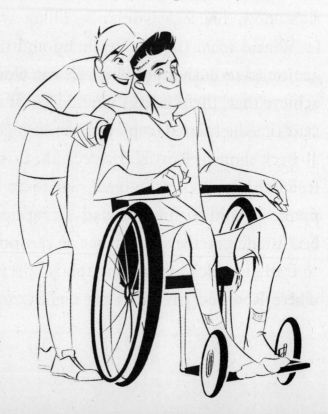

much changed since the operation that had turned his family's life upside down.

Roy's dad managed a half-smile, then he raised his right arm, signalling he wanted to go to the toilet. Roy helped his dad into his wheelchair. With only the right side of Danny Race's body working, Roy needed to take the weight of his dad's left side, putting his dad's arm around his shoulder to ease him into his chair.

Wheeling Dad out of the bedroom to the bathroom, Roy told him about Johnny Dexter scouting for Melchester Rovers. He saw his dad's eyes light up. Danny Race had watched Rovers home and away for decades, driving a minibus full of fellow fans all over the country, hundreds of thousands of miles. He had written the Rovers fanzine, *Melodrama*, and even been chairman of the supporters' club. There was no one in the city who had been more Melchester Rovers than Roy's dad.

Until the spring he was diagnosed with a brain tumour.

Until he'd been scheduled for an operation.

Until the operation went wrong.

The good news was Roy's dad had survived.

The bad news was, by the time he came out of hospital, he was paralysed down his left side, meaning he couldn't use his left arm or left leg. Even the left side of his face was immobile. And he couldn't speak. Or type. Or text. Or find the words he used to find so easily.

Roy's dad said the occasional word. But it was rare.

With the help of the local council, they'd had the whole bathroom refitted at home. And a stairlift put in too. Carers were coming to look after Roy's dad during the day when no one could be there to look after him. They were coping. It was easier for Roy. He was strong enough to take his Dad's weight. His sister was still a bit too young to manage on her own.

After they'd finished in the bathroom, Roy guided his dad into the chairlift, talking all the time about the Kelburn United game, saying this was their chance to get a first win of the season, after two straight defeats.

This was, in fact, Roy and his dad's first home game of the season. They'd missed the first two home games because Danny wasn't ready to go out.

Downstairs, Roy's sister joined them for breakfast. Roxanne was fourteen and feisty. She had short brown hair and a round face. She was clever at school. She loved football. And she hated being called Roxanne. Everyone called her Rocky.

Rocky sat up close to her dad, helping

him to pour out his cereal. She looked at Roy and shook her head and tutted.

'What?' Roy asked.

'You're still sweating,' Rocky laughed.

'I've been running.'

'I know. And it's... well, it's pretty disgusting, Roy.'

'I had a shower,' Roy replied through a mouthful of cereal.

'Did you?' Rocky looked confused.

'Yeah.'

'Couldn't you find the soap?'

'Yeah.' Roy glared at Rocky. He heard his dad stifle a laugh.

Rocky sniffed the air and grinned. 'If you say so. You still smell like a pig.'

Roy noticed that Dad was watching them, hoping for more entertainment.

But it was late. Roy stood up.

'I've got college,' he said. 'I'll see you this

afternoon, Dad.'

Dad put his thumb up.

'Dave's coming at six to take us to the match,' Roy said.

Another raised thumb.

'I wish Roxanne could come,' Roy grinned. 'Such a shame it's a school night and you'll miss our first game of the season. You must feel so frustrated.'

Roy ducked as a spoon hit the wall behind him. He left the kitchen grinning. He just couldn't wait to watch his first game of the season.

In the hall outside, Roy laced his trainers. He sensed Rocky standing over him.

'I need to talk to you about something,' his sister said.

Roy looked at his watch and shook his head. 'I'm late. I'll miss my bus.'

'I need your help.'

'Ask Mum,' Roy suggested.

'I can't ask Mum. She's always working. Or looking after dad. Or too tired. I don't want to hassle her. Come on, Roy.'

Roy stood up and looked at his watch again. Late. He was late.

'Later,' he said. 'Can't now.'

He could see his sister looked more sad than cross. Roy sighed. 'We'll talk about it later,' he said. 'I promise.' Then he was off running. Again.

THE DOUBLE DECKER edged out of the bus station and accelerated into three lanes of city centre traffic. This was Roy's second week going to college on the bus. He liked it. A lot.

For ten years he'd walked from home to school knowing everyone and everyone knowing him, doing lessons he didn't always enjoy. Now he travelled three miles by bus to college to study with people from all over town to learn about exactly what he wanted.

Sport.

Roy had always done alright at school,

usually tried hard, got okay results. But the course he was doing now was amazing. It was a BTEC National Diploma in Sport. Studying how to be a coach, how to get a job in sport, how sports clubs work, and physiology too.

As Roy stretched his legs out, still feeling a tightness from his early-morning fitness session, his phone pinged.

Blackie: You heard about Mel youth trials?

Blackie was Roy's best mate. Or used to be. Roy wondered what Blackie was doing right now. Pretty much every day of those ten years walking to school, Roy had been side by side with Blackie, his next door neighbour, his best mate, his footballing wingman. But now Blackie was in London. South London. Miles away and living with his mum who'd moved house to live with an airline pilot.

Roy: **Yeah. Dexter's coming to watch us next week.**
Blackie: **You'll kill it, Roy. Seen the news about Hugo?**

Roy wondered what Blackie was on about. Hugo was his favourite player outside Melchester Rovers. And his dad's. Roy had read the player's autobiography out loud to his dad whilst he was recovering from his operation in hospital.

Roy: **No. What?**
Blackie: **I'll let you find out for yourself.**

Roy frowned and leafed through the free *Metro* newspaper he'd picked up at the front of the bus. He liked reading the sports pages and sometimes had time for the news. As he scanned the sports stories, Roy heard the voice of a girl a couple of seats behind him. And the sound of another girl laughing. Roy didn't look round, fighting the instinct to see who it was and what they were laughing about.

The main headline was Tynecaster United's ambition to win all four trophies this season.

Roy shuddered. There were two teams in his city. Melchester Rovers. And Tynecaster United. Roy's family had always supported Melchester Rovers. His dad had been there in person when they'd last won the European Cup.

But times had changed. Now Melchester had fallen hard and fast to League Two. Tynecaster were in the Champions League.

If Tynecaster won all four trophies it would do Roy's head in. He tried not to be bothered that Tynecaster had been bought by a multi-billionaire, or that they had the pick of the top players in the country and were getting better and better every year. But he *was* bothered. Really bothered. So bothered that it hurt.

But when he saw what was written in the newspaper, the pain was almost too much.

WORLD PLAYER OF THE YEAR TO JOIN TYNECASTER

Hugo set to join Melchester's top team for record £176M

Roy folded the paper and snapped it down onto his knee. Not that. This was the ultimate nightmare. His favourite world player. His favourite FIFA player. Signing for *them*.

His head swimming, Roy stared out of the window, then back at his newspaper, where he noticed a small article about Melchester Rovers. Melchester never got column inches now they were in League Two, so he assumed it was bad news.

He was right.

MEL PARK IN THE DARK

Melchester Rovers may be forced to sell their top players to avoid bankruptcy. Rumours are the fallen giants of English football could collapse before Christmas. One club official suggested the club soon won't have the money to turn the floodlights on for night matches. Rovers play Kelburn United at home tonight, still searching for their first points of the season.

Roy felt a jumble of mixed emotions. Fear that Melchester Rovers would go bust and close down. Excitement for tonight's game. Then a new feeling. Something that took him by surprise. A wave of sadness washing over him. He had just realised that this was the first time his dad would *not* be taking him to Mel Park. He'd been going to the football with his dad since he was born. Every game. From the age of nine days to sixteen years. His dad leading him to Mel Park. His dad handing him his season ticket outside the gate, then taking it back off him on the inside.

That would never happen again.

Because now Roy would be the one taking his dad to the football.

Roy stared out of the window at a row of retail units and warehouses, pushing the pain away as they came close to Tynecastle's immense new stadium. He noticed raindrops starting to blur the windows of the bus and closed his eyes for a moment. The girl behind was speaking louder now.

'... that dump... it's not a real stadium... no soul.... no real fans... it's rubbish...'

Roy snapped out of his gloom and smiled. Roy liked what he heard. Who *was* this girl?

'I mean...' she went on, '...six years ago this place was the city sewage works... think about it... decades of Melchester's sewage have passed through the soil... no wonder the grass doesn't grow and they have to re-turf it every summer...'

Roy couldn't stop himself laughing. Desperate to look round and see who the voice belonged to, he glanced over his shoulder, still grinning. A girl was staring back at him. She had long red hair. Her skin was pale. Roy recognised her from college. In the café. In the library. He'd seen her all over the place, now he thought of it. She had large eyes. Roy couldn't tell if they were blue or green. But that didn't matter. It was her voice and her words and her sense of humour that right now appealed to him.

Roy swallowed and stared back at his newspaper. His heart was hammering. And not just because of the football.

BACK HOME. AFTER college, some hours later, Roy put on a pair of jeans, his Melchester top and a hoodie that was getting a bit small for him. He'd not mentioned that his clothes were too small to his mum: she had more to worry about than buying clothes for him. Sitting on his bed, he tied his trainer laces and looked at his official Rovers team poster on the back of his bedroom door and grinned.

This was it. Tonight. Him and his dad's first home match of the new football season. Against Kelburn United.

Roy studied the players on the poster.

He knew them all off by heart, of course. Some old faces from last season. Others, newly signed players who he'd only seen in action from last season onine. Those were the players that gave him hope. Some of the goals the new striker from Lithuania had scored! Amazing! And the pace of that winger they'd signed from the champions of Cyprus!

The best news of all was that the club had got rid of last season's disastrous manager and brought in a new boss. And it wasn't just any boss. It was none other than Kevin 'Mighty' Mouse, a club legend from when Melchester were the best team in the country, in Europe, the world.

Roy felt hope. Wasn't it better to have ex-players in charge? Men who understood the club? Men who loved the club? Of course it was! Roy clenched his fists.

Now he turned his attention to getting his dad ready for his first game since the operation. That was the real challenge. Mum was out at work and Rocky was staying round Grandma's overnight whilst everyone else was out. Roy would have to sort this one out by himself.

As he got Dad dressed and into his wheelchair, Roy talked about what he'd read in the newspaper that morning.

'Hugo's signing for them,' he said.

Dad nodded and put his thumb down.

'How could he?'

Dad shrugged his right shoulder.

That was the sum of their conversation.

DAVE, DAD'S OLD work mate, picked them up at six o'clock. Dave was a taxi driver now and had one of those taxis with a ramp, making it easier for Roy's dad to board the taxi.

Before Roy pushed him out of the front door he stopped to tie the red and yellow Melchester scarf around his Dad's neck. His dad winked. Roy had done the right thing. But Roy still felt sad. His dad didn't say *It's going to be a good season, Roy* or *What do you think the score will be, kid?*

But Roy knew exactly what his dad would be thinking as the wheelchair bumped down the concrete garden path and into Dave's cab. So Roy decided to answer the unasked questions.

'First win of the season, today, Dad. This will be the turning point. The only way is up from now on.'

Roy sat in the back of the taxi opposite Dad. Dave asked Roy about playing for Grimroyd. But he was quieter than usual.

Roy reckoned that Dave was nervous about seeing his old friend in a wheelchair and that was why he was struggling.

Dave filled the latest silence telling them about a rumour he'd heard in the pub last night. Melchester were going to sell off all their best players before the transfer window closed. Anyone they could make money from. Anyone on wages over £50,000 a year.

'Who told you that?' Roy asked, guessing that was what his dad also wanted to know.

'A mate. His daughter works part time in the club office. Knows everything that's going on.'

It echoed the story Roy had read in the newspaper on the bus.

Roy tried to forget the rumours. He still wanted to enjoy being at Mel Park tonight.

Dave dropped them off at the disabled entrance at the corner of stadium.

'Thanks, Dave,' Roy said.

'Any time you need me,' Dave said. 'Just text. Got to get Melchester's number one fan to the match!'

Roy pushed his dad's wheelchair through a set of gates with Melchester Rovers spelled out in wrought iron, showing their wheelchair area pass to the woman on the gate. Into the tunnel that disappeared into the bowels of the stadium. At the entrance to the tunnel, Roy noticed a small group of people looking over at his dad, one pointing.

'Is that Danny Race?' he heard someone gasp. 'What's happened to him?' The voices carried easily in the confines of the tunnel.

'I heard cancer,' another said.

Roy winced. He knew that if he could hear them gossiping, then his dad would be able to as well.

He pushed his dad's wheelchair a little

58

faster, out of the shadow and cold air of the tunnel, where he was directed to the right. The great rectangle of grass ahead seemed to glow in the warm evening sun. Roy felt a buzz of excitement. He loved evening matches early in the season. No scars or worn out patches on the grass. The smell of the grass after the pitch had been watered.

'Look at that!' Roy gasped, putting his hand on his dad's shoulder. 'It's perfect.'

Dad put his good hand onto Roy's hand and squeezed.

A man was working on the pitch, wearing a threadbare old Rovers top. Seeing them, the man stuck his fork into the pitch and walked over to Roy and his dad.

'I hear you've had a rough summer, Danny,' he said.

Roy's dad put his thumb up, tried to smile. It was Robbo: the club groundsman.

'We all heard about it,' Robbo went on. 'And, for what it's worth, mate, I'm very sorry what's happened to you. But I'm glad to see you back.'

Roy's dad put his thumb up again. He'd always got on with Robbo.

'So, come with me, Danny Race,' Robbo said. 'Because I've saved you a spot with great views and a fresh coat of paint just this week in your honour, so that I could make it the best seat in the house.'

Robbo looked at Roy. 'May I?' he asked, taking the wheelchair off Roy and pushing his dad to the front of the main stand, where there was a space for a wheelchair marked out in yellow lines, a seat next to it for Roy. Right next to the home dugout.

Roy let Robbo take the wheelchair and followed his dad to their new seats. He struggled not to grin. It was hard adapting to this new life with his dad. But these pitch side seats were definitely going to make it a bit easier.

Roy stood up with the rest of the crowd as they sensed the players were about to come onto the pitch. But Roy noticed that, even though kick off was imminent, three of the stands were still only half full. The fourth stand was empty. When his dad had first brought him to Mel Park all four stands had always been full, not an empty seat to be seen. Now, overall, more seats were empty than taken.

But Roy ignored the emptiness. He was here to support Rovers and that was what he would do.

Roy loved his new seat at Mel Park. He was so close to the action he only needed to reach out and his foot would be on the turf. It might be an old-style stadium, stands stuck together, each one built in a different decade, but Roy preferred that to the new stadiums that most teams played in now.

As the players came out of the tunnel to the sound of the club song, the new manager appeared behind them and strode towards the home dugout. A muted cheer filled Mel Park, the fans welcoming their former player, now manager, still hoping he could make Melchester great again. But beneath that cheer Roy could sense something new in the atmosphere: anxiety, worry, panic even.

As Kevin 'Mighty' Mouse waved to acknowledge the applause of the fans in each of the three stands, Roy watched him. He

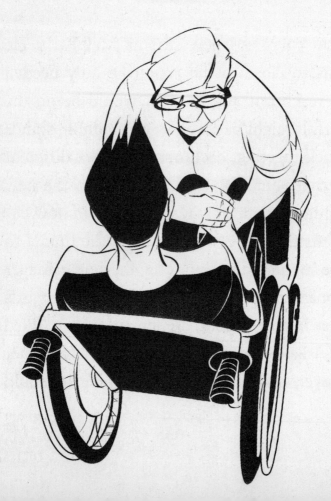

was short and a little overweight, but he still looked like the small, powerful striker Dad had shown Roy playing in old clips online.

To Roy's surprise, the manager's next move was to come straight up to Roy's dad and shake his hand. Kevin 'Mighty' Mouse knelt down and spoke quietly to Roy's dad.

'Anything I can do, let me know. Okay, Danny?'

Roy got a pat on the shoulder too. He was stunned. What a great man! Here was the manager of a team that was adrift at the foot of League Two with no wins or even draws in four games and he'd taken the time to greet Roy's dad.

No wonder he was a club legend.

The atmosphere was building more positively towards kick off. The regular chant of *Rovers! Rovers! Rovers!* echoing round the old stadium. A thousand conversations about the game building into a roar with the home team kicking off.

Roy grinned. He loved the feeling at kick-off. Excitement. Anticipation. Hope. He yelled out 'Come on Rovers!' at the top of his voice.

During the first few minutes of the game Roy found himself on his feet, then sitting down, then on his feet again. When Melchester had possession of the ball, Roy felt himself change the angle of his body, so he could take the pass, then lift himself off the seat to make a header. It was madness, but he always did this. His dad used to tell him to relax, that he was there to watch the game, not play it, but Roy was so involved in the game that he needed to twitch his body around to be ready for the ball.

Maybe one day.

Just two minutes into the game, the

Melchester keeper hoofed a ball up the pitch, where it bounced, sending all three Melchester forwards plus all but one of the midfielders charging into the Kelburn United penalty area.

It was a chance, but a chance Melchester didn't seize. Kelburn won the ball back. And now it was clear that Melchester had over-committed, as, suddenly, four Kelburn players were advancing on the home goal, against only two remaining Melchester defenders.

Roy put his hands to his face. He could see what was about to happen as the players scrambled to get back to their positions.

Two more passes, a striker one-on-one with the Melchester keeper and, as the noise of the away fans filled the stadium, Roy saw the ball bouncing in the back of the Melchester net.

0-1.

Roy felt like he'd had a punch to the stomach. Three minutes into his first game of the season and they were losing already. He watched Mighty Mouse leap from his seat, yelling and pointing. He saw Johnny Dexter on the bench too, frowning, shaking his head.

Not a good start.

Then, after half an hour, another goal for Kelburn.

0-2.

Mel Park was silent after that, the hope well and truly gone. Roy could hear the thump of boot on ball, the shouts between the players, like the game was being played in an empty stadium. The evening sun had disappeared behind the Tom Tully stand and the slight breeze saw several people putting their coats on, even though it was only early September.

In the silence Roy could hear voices from the home dugout. Kevin Mouse talking to Johnny Dexter.

'How's the youth scouting going?'

'Steady,' Dexter replied. 'Got some good tips.'

Mighty Mouse shook his head. 'We might need those youngsters sooner than I first thought.'

At half time, Roy moved in close to his dad. 'Did you hear Mouse and Dexter talking?'

Dad shook his head.

'They were talking about needing youth players. Soon. Do you think they're going to sell all the first team players like Dave said?'

Dad put his thumb up. But frowned.

'That's thumbs up, but not in a good way,' Roy suggested.

69

Dad nodded.

Roy stared at the pitch: the first half had not given him much to feel good about. He thought of certain people he knew at college. Tynecaster fans. Two of them in particular would be on his back in the morning, laughing and gloating.

He hated that. But he'd deal with it when it happened.

The second half was no better than the first. Roy saw how cautiously Melchester were playing. Just when they needed to hit back. Roy knew how weak the Kelburn defenders were on the ball. All Melchester had to do was pressure them when they had possession and they'd make mistakes. If Melchester could score then it'd be 2-1. Then the game's energy would swing in their favour. Melchester just needed one goal to kick start the recovery.

'PRESS THE BALL!' Mighty Mouse shouted. 'When they've got it, PRESS!'

Roy was pleased the Melchester manager agreed with him. As he watched the substitutes being pushed out of the dugout to warm up on the side lines, Roy imagined he was one of them. Stripping off his Melchester Rovers tracksuit, stretching and shuttle-running up and down the touchline, clapping back at the fans who applauded him.

He could do it right now.

He had a club top on, even if he'd not had a new one for three seasons. Roy wondered if he joined them on the side lines would anyone stop him? He had always had this fantasy that he'd be at a match and Melchester would be a player down and desperate for anyone to come on and make up the numbers. And he'd be there in his top. He'd get thrown onto the pitch and then he'd score goal after goal and make everything alright.

Roy's dreams were shattered to pieces by the sight of the Kelburn striker running past, his finger on his lips, mocking the Rovers fans as he celebrated.

0-3.

Another goal. One Roy had missed with his daydreaming.

Game over. There was no coming back.

Roy looked at his dad. His dad had his eyes closed. But he wasn't asleep. His right fist was clenched so hard that his knuckles were bone-white. His jaw was rigid. But, unlike in previous seasons, Dad was not shouting and letting out all his frustration.

How awful must that be? One of the best bits about going to the football was shouting your head off when it was going wrong, Roy thought.

But Danny Race would never shout again.

So, with that thought troubling him, Roy got up and shouted. The loudest, longest, most heart-felt howl of frustration that had ever come out of his mouth.

IT WAS DARK by the time Mum got back from the care home.

Mum had four evening shifts a week. She went out to clean at some local shops and banks first thing in the morning as well. She was always on call for social services too.

Roy was playing FIFA for his dad when she came in. Over the summer, he'd taken Melchester Rovers from League Two to the Premier League in three seasons. Now they were top of the Premier League. Dad loved watching Melchester on FIFA. Roy usually did extra commentaries for him. Although tonight – still hurting from the defeat at Mel Park – they were sitting in silence.

Mum put her head round the door. She was tall with shoulder-length blonde hair. Father and son looked up at her without speaking.

'Oh dear,' Mum twisted her mouth. 'Bad was it? Three or four?'

'Three,' Roy said, knowing that his mum took their feelings about their football club seriously to a point. But, if they went on too much about it, she'd get sick of them and start to tease them.

'Nil?' Mum asked.

'Nil.'

'I'm sorry,' Mum said, as if she'd just heard news of the death of a close friend.

Roy paused his game and stood up. 'Need a run,' he said.

'Bit late, isn't it?' Mum said.

'I need to, Mum.'

'Okay,' Mum said.

Outside the room, Roy sat at the foot of the stairs and put his trainers on.

'How did you get on at the football?' Mum asked in a soft voice. 'With your dad? Was it okay?'

'It *was*, actually,' Roy said. 'Dave gave us a lift. Robbo the groundsman was great with Dad. Mighty Mouse even came and had a chat.'

'I knew they'd look after him.' Mum smiled sadly. 'Get out on your run. You've had a tough night. You're a good lad.'

IT WAS SUPPOSED to be an easy run without his ball. Just something to loosen up with ahead of Grimroyd's Moor Cup semi-final the next day. But Roy found himself running harder and harder. Ankles cracking as he hit the uneven cobbles. Harder still when he was on the flat alongside the ill-lit canal. Almost at a sprint. It was like he wanted it to hurt.

Within seven minutes he found himself back at Mel Park.

It was a clear night. No cloud. A full moon. The floodlights were off, so Robbo would be done patching up the pitch.

Roy did one lap of the perimeter of the stadium, up through the main car park, along the fence where the training ground backed onto the Tom Tully Stand.

The hole in the fence from last season was still there. Roy didn't hesitate, ducking in through it, making sure he didn't catch himself on the loose wires. He skirted the training pitch, a large patch of shadow leaving him invisible as he reached the corner of the Tom Tully Stand and the North Bank.

Like the fence, the door was old and not as secure as it needed to be. Roy pulled the wooden door so that its chain was tight, then he slipped through the gap.

He was in.

Mel Park to himself.

Roy jogged to the front of the main stand. There was no lighting, but the moon was casting a pale light onto the steps and the red and yellow painted wooden fold-up seats.

Roy wasn't there to sit there and mope. He wanted to chase away the gloom that had been troubling him all evening.

Seventy-two steps to the back of the stand. Roy took them in threes. Twenty-four strides as fast as he could, legs burning, chest imploding, seeing off the memory of those people talking about his dad as if he wasn't there. Then a slow jog down. Slow as he could, because as soon as he hit the bottom step it was hard up the steps again.

Faster the second time. Feeling his legs seizing up. Trying not to think about how his dad couldn't let out his anger when the third goal went in.

Roy did a set of ten ups and downs before he sat at the back of the main stand and allowed himself to look around Mel Park. That was proper training. What coach had been talking about.

Roy smiled.

He had some reasons to be happy. He had Mel Park all to himself. A semi-final to maybe play in the next day, if he hadn't been dropped. And then... there was that girl on the bus.

Turning up for the next Moor Cup match after a full day at college, Roy had something new to deal with. Since he started playing football for the Under-7s all the way through to the Under-16s he'd always been the first name on the team sheet. Not today. Today Roy had been dropped.

'I might bring you on in the second half,' Yunis told him. 'All being well.'

'Yes, Coach,' Roy said, then went to jog up and down the pitch to stay supple.

The semi-final of the Moor Cup – Grimroyd v Erringden FC – kicked off in impossible evening heat, and, unlike the first game, this was not tight.

It was open.

Very open.

So open that it was 3-3 at half time.

Roy had worked out why the game was like that. The problem was defending. *Bad* defending. Their opponents' back four were not great, backing off so that they were lined up next to their keeper, trying to block shots rather than tackle. That struck Roy as weird. But not as weird as Grimroyd's defence – because Lofty was awful. Truly awful. Clearly to blame for all three goals Grimroyd conceded.

At half time Yunis did what needed doing, even before the players were sitting down, taking on water.

'Lofty, you're tired, or something. Either way, you're coming off. Roy, I want you on.'

Lofty nodded and then winked at Roy.

'I want five in defence with Gus and Finn to play as wing backs. I think we're fitter than Erringden and their full backs are weak, so I'd like to see the ball moving up the wings and three players in the box on the end of crosses. Roy, you need to push yourself into that penalty area every time Finn or Gus starts a run. You've got more freedom this week. Use it or lose it. Got it?'

'Yes, Coach.'

Roy felt good. He was on. Yunis was giving him the chance to play the game his way, as an individual.

Roy settled into his position on the pitch. He noticed that the defender marking him had a tattoo that emerged from the top of his football shirt up to his throat. But he wasn't distracted. He had his instructions, waiting for the ball to go out to the wingbacks, then running in parallel, staying onside as they raided the Erringden half. Other than that he could do what he wanted and read the game for himself.

But, wherever Roy went, the tattooed defender was always there. So close sometimes Roy could smell his stale sweaty odour. Sometimes, when the referee wasn't watching, the defender nudged Roy, pushed him, clipped his ankle.

But, as the second half wore on Roy's marker began to tire. Roy began to increase the number of runs he made, even if they were pointless, hoping to tire his defender out as he was forced to track Roy.

Roy remembered what Yunis had said after the first game. Be more vocal. Demand the ball. That he didn't deserve the ball unless he demanded it.

'VINNY!' Roy shouted, having moved

into a position where he had plenty of space ahead of him. 'HERE!'

Roy saw Vinny look up, then, play a high fast ball at an angle that was speeding to the far side of the Erringden penalty area.

Roy took off. Fast. The tattooed defender was out of it, shattered. But two other Erringden players were closing in on Roy, one side by side with him, ready to shoulder him out of the way. Roy didn't wait to be unbalanced as he came side by side with the defender. Instead, he pushed into him, shoulder to shoulder, then took the impetus of the collision to drive into the penalty area and hit a volley hard and clean with his left foot.

The ball angled across the keeper who reached to touch it round the post. But there was too much pace on it. There was no saving that rocket.

GOAL!

Roy stood stunned. He'd done it. Scored his first goal for Grimroyd Under-18s. He took the handshakes and pats on the back of his team mates as he jogged back to take position for the restart. He was thrilled. He'd scored a goal. But not just any goal. He'd scored a volley. The summer spent practicing had paid off.

ROY AND LOFTY sat on the far side of the pitch staring out across the town, legs outstretched, muscles aching from the effort of the game. A 4-3 win, meaning Grimroyd had made it to the Moor Cup Final. The rest of the team – and Yunis – had gone home. It was just the two friends now. The sun was weaker. Just right for sitting on the grass and talking.

Not that Roy nor Lofty were saying much as they stretched.

Roy ran his eyes up and down the rows of terraced-house streets that ran from the top to the bottom of the hill in neat lines. But Roy knew that Lofty was looking further across the valley, a frown hardening his face.

Roy understood the frown. Lofty was still hurting. The lights of Tynecaster's twenty-first century space ship stadium were on, no doubt reminding Lofty of what he was no longer part of.

'How long were you there?' Roy asked gently.

Lofty exhaled. 'I was six when they scouted me, so that's ten years, I suppose...'

'You played so well today,' Roy said.

Lofty shook his head.

'You did,' Roy insisted, but he knew it wasn't true.

'I was rubbish, Roy, and I'm done with football,' Lofty said.

'What?'

'I don't care about it anymore.' Lofty faced Roy, his eyes reflecting the lights from the Tynecaster stadium.

Roy leaned over and grabbed Lofty by the front of his tracksuit top and pulled it tight at the zip.

'No,' he barked.

Lofty – taller, stronger and harder than Roy – raised an eyebrow, but Roy kept his grip tight.

'Tynecaster are the worst club for young local players.' Roy stared into Lofty's eyes. 'More than half their squad are from abroad.

They don't invest in youth. Everyone knows that. They just spend. Rovers would snap you up.'

Lofty shook his head and ignored the compliment. 'All clubs are like that now Roy,' he said. 'No one wants local players anymore and, even if they did, I don't want them.'

'But Melch…' Roy started, but he was interrupted.

'I told you, I'm done with football,' Lofty said. 'And anyway… isn't that your sister?'

Roy looked up. Lofty was right. Rocky was walking across the pitch. She had a look on her face that Roy couldn't work out.

Suddenly Roy was worried. Dad? Was Dad okay?

He ran over to Rocky. 'Everything okay?'

'You said we'd talk,' Rocky said.

Roy put his hand to his forehead. 'I'm sorry. We will.'

'It's important. This thing I want to talk about. And you're never in... and I used to talk to Dad about stuff that worried me and I can't talk to Mum. And I can't talk to Dad...'

Rocky stopped talking. She stared across the wide and empty moor.

'I know,' Roy said. 'I'm sorry.'

They sat where Roy and Lofty had been talking. The grass was short and flattened.

'What's up?' Roy asked.

'I was watching all the games on the moor. You didn't see me.'

'Okay,' Roy said.

'And I noticed something about them all.'

'Go on.'

'No,' Rocky folded her arms. 'What do think I you noticed?'

Roy noted the change in tone of Rocky's voice. No longer needy, she was now coming across as angry. Roy tried to think what it was about the games on the moor that had made his sister angry. He was struggling.

'You don't see it, do you?' Rocky asked.

Roy shrugged. 'Just tell me.' He was thinking hard now. What had she spotted that she didn't like? Had she heard people swearing? Was that going to bother her?

'You want me to point out the obvious?' Rocky said finally.

Roy nodded.

'No women. No girls. Just men. Just boys. I'm just as good as you at football. But where do I go to play? There are no girls' teams on this moor. No opportunities for me. It's rubbish. It's not fair. And I need you to do something about it.'

Roy stared at Rocky. 'Me?'

'Yes, you.'

'Look I get what you mean, Rocky. And you're right. It's wrong. But what can I do?'

94

'That's what everyone says. My teachers at school: what can we do? The council sport centre: what can we do? Now you: what can I do?'

Roy swallowed.

'So tell me,' he said. 'I'll try and help. But what... I mean... really... what can I do?'

'You can do what Dad would have done,' Rocky said.

'Roy?'

The voice was familiar and rang down the long corridor at college, as Roy shouldered through three hundred students shuffling to their 9 a.m. lectures. The day after Roy's game. Two days after Melchester had lost at home.

'Roy? Where are you *racing* off to?'

Roy heard laughter. It was Sam Bustard. And his mate, Ben. It was always Sam Bustard. Roy stopped and turned around. He wasn't going to run away from an idiot like Sam. He would face him down. Roy had done well to keep out of his way yesterday entirely. As he faced Sam, he wondered why Sam was risking making Roy's surname into a joke.

Sam and Ben looked like brothers. Short. Pale. Unhealthy.

'Who's top of the Premier League, Race?' Sam gloated.

Roy had to decide how to play this. The bottom line was he needed to walk away on top, put Sam and Ben in their place. They were trying to make him look and feel like an idiot: Roy needed to stay calm, wait for Sam to make a mistake, like any footballing defence always made at least one.

'Tynecaster.' Roy replied in a deadpan voice.

Sam looked surprised, but went on. 'Who's bottom of League Two?'

'Melchester.' Roy smiled.

'Do you realise,' Sam went on, glancing at

Ben, 'this is the biggest possible gap we could have between our two teams. I bet there's a hundred places be...'

Roy interrupted. He'd made his first mistake. 'That's ninety-one, Bustard.'

'What?'

'Ninety-one places. There are ninety-two teams in the league.' Roy felt anger coursing through him now, a heat rising up his neck and into his head.

'Ninety-one places?' Sam scoffed.

'Don't you know anything about football?' Roy laughed. 'I mean, really?'

Roy saw something then in Sam's eyes. The smile had faded.

Sam put his hands on his hips. 'So, we're ninety-one times better than you, Race. That shows how rubbish you are. We're...'

'We?' Roy jumped on Sam's second mistake. 'Who do you mean when you say *we*? How many times have you been to see Tynecaster? Have you *ever* been?'

Sam stepped back, avoided looking into Roy's eyes. And now Roy knew he had him.

'You can't get tickets,' Sam spluttered. 'Every match is sold out. It's just season tickets. And they cost loads.'

Roy shook his head. 'No. I read about it in *Match of the Day* magazine.' The last traces of his anger had gone. He felt in control of himself. In control of this argument. Sam had just made his third mistake. 'Tynecaster have ninety per cent season tickets,' Roy said. 'Ten per cent go on sale one month before the game. Don't you know anything about your own team?'

It was all quiet in the corridor now. Dozens were stood watching Sam and Roy. This education Roy was giving Ben was better than any lecture they were likely to have today.

Then, scanning the audience, Roy saw her. The girl from the bus. She was leaning against a door frame, a smile playing on her lips. Roy swallowed and looked back at Sam. His opponent was speechless. Defeated. And now, Roy felt sorry for him.

Was it time to show mercy? To be kind?

'Look,' Roy changed the tone of his voice. 'I don't mind if Tynecaster do well. But what does my head in is Tynecaster fans who are top of the league and in the Champions League still going on and on about us, even though Tynecaster are the best in the country. They've just signed the best player in world.'

'Hugo,' Sam spluttered. 'We signed Hugo from…'

Roy nodded. 'Well done. Yes, Hugo. Even though you've got all that going on, even though Tynecaster are living the dream, all their fans want to do is talk about Melchester. Why is that?'

Sam scowled. He'd seen the audience around them now and knew he had lost. His face was pink and he was rocking from foot to foot.

'Because it's funny,' he said.

Roy heard a few claps. A couple of cheers. He imagined that most of the students watching were probably Tynecaster fans, even if they weren't real ones. They might turn on Roy at any moment, however right he was. He needed to be careful to still come out on top.

Roy shook his head. 'No,' he said, pushing past Sam. 'Tynecaster still go on about Melchester because, deep deep down in the bottom of their hearts and minds, Tynecaster still feel inferior to Melchester and they know – even deeper down still – that one day we'll be back.'

Sam started laughing. But it was a forced hollow laugh. Roy could see he'd hit home.

Roy walked away from Sam and Ben. Past their audience, still grinning. And past the girl from the bus, who looked him in the eye and smiled. Roy smiled back, but that was all he could manage. What he needed was a reason to talk to her.

THURSDAY NIGHT TRAINING, three days before the Moor Cup final. Even though it was seven in the evening, the air was hot. The grass was yellow and dry. The soil hard. Roy took in the noise of footballers arriving. Shouts. Laughter. Balls being struck. Car doors slamming. It felt weird that some of his teammates had arrived in their own cars.

There was no sign of Lofty. Roy was starting to worry that he was going to live up to his promise and give up football. That he had really meant it.

After warming up and some basic drills – passing, heading, shuttle-runs – Yunis addressed the players. They were to play a game. Twenty minutes. Seven-a-side. On a half-sized pitch.

'I want you to push it. This team we're up against on Saturday are tough. Tough and very physical.' Yunis glanced at Roy. 'I want you to prepare for that now. Nothing that's going to put anyone out of the game, but we need it hard. If we win on Saturday, we've achieved more than this team has ever done. We might as well prepare for it right.'

Roy looked up to see that he had been pitched against Vinny. He frowned. But then, slowly, his frown turned into a smile. He had understood what Yunis was doing. The fact that he was playing against Vinny wasn't a catastrophe: it was an opportunity.

What had Yunis asked of him? Be more physical. That's what he'd said. So he would be. He already felt like his extra training had made him stronger and fitter. And he was out to prove it.

The first time Roy challenged Vinny for the ball, he led with his shoulder and felt Vinny's chest crunch as he hit him. Vinny staggered, trying to keep his balance, but fell on all fours, scowling at Roy.

Yunis gave a foul. Against Roy.

A second clash came quickly. Roy took the ball with his back to goal, Vinny just behind him, his knee digging into Roy's thigh hard. Instead of recoiling, Roy pushed back, forcing Vinny to hack at the ball between Roy's legs, but giving Roy time to drop his shoulder and play the ball wide.

The third time they sparred, Roy led again with his shoulder, side by side. Roy was amazed that he'd kept his balance and had pushed Vinny off the ball. Not stopping to think about it, he ran on, the ball bouncing high ahead of him on the hard surface. Roy watched it rise, then fall, then he hit it hard with his left. A half-volley of the side of his left boot.

It screamed into the back of the net, tearing the ties, the net flapping loose. The force of the shot caused Roy to stumble and fall.

And then a hand came down to pull him up.

Vinny pulled Roy until they were face to face. The defender glowered.

'Make sure you do that in the final on Saturday and I might forgive you for making me look like a clown.'

AFTER TRAINING, ROY sat down at the edge of the pitch for a drink. Cheap squash with salt in it. Nothing fancy. He couldn't afford isotonic drinks: not four times a week. Roy took his phone out of his bag and texted Lofty.

Roy: **Where are you?**

Lofty:

Roy: **Eh?**

Lofty: **Basketball. I joined a team.**

Roy: **But what about Grimroyd?**

Roy: **I told you. I'm done with football.**

Roy frowned.

'Basketball?' he said to himself. 'What was the point of that?'

Then Yunis was next to him, sweating heavily in the heat as he slumped down on the dry grass.

'First sign of madness,' Coach gasped.

'What?' Roy said. 'Running at your age?'

'Funny,' Yunis laughed and cuffed Roy's head. 'No. Talking to yourself. You're the crazy one. Anyway, you did good today, Roy. Really good. I told Vinny to harass you, you know? I asked him to be tough on you. That's all I wanted from him. But you were much more physical today. You matched him – and some. I'm pleased with your progress. Well done.'

'Thanks, Coach.'

'Johnny Dexter's coming on Saturday, you know?'

'Hardman?' Roy whispered, barely able to believe it.

'The man himself. He's not sending any old nobody. I've told him about you and Peak, you see. I've told him you two – and maybe a couple of the others – are worth a look. Because you are, Roy. You in particular.'

Roy couldn't believe what he was hearing. 'Really? I'm not too young?'

Coach shook his head. 'Come on Roy,' he said. 'Do you believe that?'

'I'm 16. Am I really strong enough?'

'Age is one thing. Power is another. But,

we both know you've got it. And that volley? A beauty.'

Roy stared at the grass. Was this real? A scout coming to see him? Him and Lofty? He wasn't sure if he should mention Lofty to Yunis. That he wasn't coming to the final.

But Yunis pre-empted him.

'So where is he, then? Peak?'

Roy was torn now. Wasn't it up to Lofty to tell Coach he'd quit? And maybe Roy had misunderstood Lofty. Maybe he'd come to the final if he knew he'd be scouted.

'He couldn't make it tonight,' Roy said. It wasn't a lie. But it wasn't telling Coach everything.

'Saturday, then?' Coach said. 'The final? He's coming for that?'

Roy shrugged. And, as he stalled for time, he had an idea. He'd go to the basketball court. Now. He'd tell Lofty about Johnny

Dexter. Then it'd all be alright. How would Lofty be able to resist being scouted by Melchester Rovers?

'I'll go and see him, Coach,' Roy said. 'I'll let you know.'

THE INDOOR COURT felt alien to Roy. It was like a school sports hall, but with a massive bank of seats down one side of the court. Every thud of the ball and shout from the coaches echoed harshly in his ears. Roy was definitely more of an outdoor sportsman than indoor.

Most of the players wore vests and light brightly-coloured trainers. There was a lot of colour. And the scent of bodies doing sport without fresh moor air to blow the smell away.

Basketball.

It wasn't for Roy. The main reason was not the airlessness, but that fact that nobody was kicking balls. He could see four balls being played with and none had been kicked. Roy felt twitchy. It just wasn't… *right*.

Roy had been trying to think of a way to persuade Lofty that he should come to the final and get himself seen by Melchester

Rovers. He'd gone over a hundred sentences in his head. But so far he had nothing that he thought was any good.

After a few long minutes of Roy watching the large orange ball being tossed around the hall, Lofty was replaced and he came off the court, sweat running down his chest and arms. Lofty looked different to normal. There was something about him, the way he moved. His eyes were bright. He was grinning. His legs and arms were just... it was hard to say... Then Roy understood. Lofty looked *happy*.

'What did you think?' Lofty asked Roy, jogging up the steps.

Roy wanted to say it was rubbish. But he held that back.

'Roy?'

'Great,' Roy said.

Lofty nodded squinting at Roy. 'Yeah?'

Roy looked down. 'I know it's important to you. So it's good. Yeah?'

Lofty nodded. 'Cheers, mate.'

Roy felt himself blush. What was this? He hated lying. And he knew he had to pretend to like basketball and that the only way to persuade Lofty to come back to football was to be respectful of his game.

But basketball? Roy thought to himself. *Really?*

'Want to shoot some?' Lofty asked.

'No.'

'No?'

'I just... I can't... I mean... What's the point... you don't get to kick it. You don't get to wrap your foot round the ball and send it across the hall. You don't get to run free. You have to stop or bounce it or whatever you have to do. I mean it's just not...' Roy stopped. He saw that three or four of the other players were looking at him now, listening, frowning.

'… football?' Lofty laughed. 'You mean it's not football?'

'I do.' Roy spoke as quietly as he could. He'd already offended half Lofty's teammates.

Lofty put his hand on Roy's shoulder and squeezed. 'That's why you're going to be a footballer, my friend. And why I'm not.'

Lofty walked down the steps back onto the basketball court. Lofty raised his hand to apologise for Roy.

'Don't you ever just want to boot it across the hall?' Roy asked.

Lofty turned to Roy and winked, as one of the other basketball players passed him a ball. Lofty caught it lightly, bounced it twice and then released it, his fingers stretching after it, like they were guiding it through the air. Roy smiled when the basketball sailed through the hoop without even touching the back board.

'Will you tell Yunis?' Roy called down to Lofty. 'Or shall I? He's expecting you for the final on Saturday.'

Lofty looked serious. 'I'll call him, Roy. Thanks for coming.'

Roy walked up the steps and out of the basketball court, Lofty's words echoing in his ears. *That's why you're going to be a footballer, Roy.*

'WILL YOU WALK me to school?'

'What?' Roy stared across the breakfast table at his sister. This was new. His sister asking him to walk her to school.

Roy, Rocky and Dad had eaten breakfast in silence. All three had gone to the Melchester match the day before. A 2-0 Sunday lunchtime defeat to one of the newly promoted teams. North Vale. A team that had been non-league three months ago.

It had been humiliating. A game Roy thought would start to turn the season round, but now Melchester were firmly bottom of the football league. To make it worse Tynecaster had won their latest game 5-0 and were even further ahead, right at the top of the Premier League.

Not a good day.

'Why do you want me to walk you to school?' Roy asked, mouth stuffed with cereal. He glanced at his dad, who winked. But Roy knew exactly why she wanted to talk to him.

'Because it's the only time I'll get to talk to you,' Rocky replied, punching him on the arm quite hard. 'Now move it.'

ONCE THEY'D SORTED Dad out in the front room with the things he needed before his carer arrived at ten – a bottle of water, some fruit and the TV remote – Roy followed his sister out of the front door. Roy was carrying his rucksack, a football bulging inside. He picked up Rocky's school bag too, but she snatched it off him.

'I can carry my own bag,' she snapped.

Roy took the ball out of his own bag threw it to his sister.

Rocky was wearing her school uniform, but also her scruffy trainers. She punted the ball ahead of them, into Roy's path.

Roy felt good. Although he didn't miss school, he did miss the walk to school. How many years had he and Rocky kicked a ball up the street, then across the far end of the Moor to school? Or had a kick about after school? And at school? It was a big part of their life. Or it had been.

Roy was overjoyed to be wearing his own clothes though, that was for sure.

'Is it fun wearing a school uniform still?' Roy said, tapping the ball against a wall so that it bounced into Rocky's path.

'Ha ha,' Rocky replied.

Roy was expecting more. Some funny remark. Some dig. But he got nothing and was now beginning to worry about Rocky. Maybe she really *did* have a problem. Maybe she wanted him to walk her to school so she could tell him about it. She certainly didn't want a bag-carrier. They walked up the long street of terraced houses to the top of the hill, the noise of the ball hitting walls and, once, off a lamppost.

The weather was warm. Rocky took her blazer off, overheating.

'School rules say you have to wear your blazer all the way to school,' Roy said helpfully.

'Shut it,' Rocky said. 'I'm not in the mood.'

They were walking along the side of the Moor now. The sun casting long black shadows off the football posts. Roy felt a lightness in his chest. The match tonight. A final. And Johnny Dexter coming. Today was a big day. He needed a bit of time to get his head round it. And, maybe then, to work out how to help his sister.

'Since you left school I don't get a game at lunchtime,' Rocky began, keeping the ball up with flicks and kicks as they walked along. 'When you were there, I did. Girls did. But now there's too many boys and they're not letting us play. I'm not playing at school. I'm not even playing with you. There are no teams at school. No teams on the Moor. I'm not whining, Roy. I want to play football. But I don't know what to do. I would have asked Dad. Before. But now I can't.'

Roy stopped. 'I'm sorry.'

'You don't need to be sorry, Roy. You need to help me.' Rocky still had complete control of the ball.

'I will.'

'When?'

'Let me have a think.'

'You said that before.'

'But I will.'

'You'd better.'

They were a couple of hundred yards from the school gate when Rocky pointed back down the road.

'Go,' she ordered, lofting the ball up for Roy to control with his head, then turning to walk alone to school.

'Look,' Roy said. 'I'll find a way to help you. I promise. Just give me some time. Okay?'

ROY WALKED ACROSS the Moor and – picking the ball up – jogged down the Terrible 200 to the bus station. He made good time, so he caught the usual 08.05 bus.

She wasn't on it.

Roy stared out of the window and thought about the Melchester match the day before, the Grimroyd final tonight, Johnny Dexter scouting, his sister and the promise he'd just made to her. And a dozen other things. He had a lot on his mind.

Roy arrived at college far too early, so he found a quiet spot on the campus with two low walls at right angles to each other. He took his ball out of his backpack and started short passing at speed, alternating the ball off each wall. Faster and faster. Trying to keep control. Honing his first touch. Never losing control.

Then he heard a voice. 'Here is Melchester Rovers' star striker, Roy Race, training. But because Melchester can't afford a training ground, he has to train against a wall.'

Roy glanced up. Ben was filming him on his phone as Sam talked.

Roy felt a flash of anger, an instinct to fight back. He'd had enough of these two idiots.

'I RECKON YOU'LL get a game for Smellchester the way you're going,' Sam said loudly, making sure it'd be heard on the film Ben was making. 'All you've got left is a bunch of cripples.'

Roy put his foot on the ball. He was staring back at Sam and Ben, trying desperately to keep his cool, hands on his hips.

His dad had once told him that it was stronger man who kept his cool rather than use violence. Roy breathed evenly and relaxed his mind. He would listen to his Dad – what his Dad used to say. He wasn't giving

Ben and Sam what they wanted: a film of him losing it. That'd be online and across college in seconds.

Roy managed to stay calm. Until Sam said what he said next.

'Did your lot all turn up in wheelchairs last night?'

Roy's face changed. He walked towards Ben, ball under his arm, bright lights around him, like fireworks, or car headlights, his brain hurting.

Roy hadn't hit anyone ever. Not once.

'What did you say?' he growled, advancing until they were face to face. He could smell Sam's sour breath. Sam had been drinking energy drinks. Roy could tell. He reeked of it. Roy never touched that rubbish.

But a voice stopped him just in time.

'He doesn't know about your dad,' the voice said. 'Sam, Roy's dad is in a wheelchair.'

Roy felt his ball being slipped gently from under his arm. A hand on his shoulder. He turned to see the girl from the bus. She took his ball. She stood between Roy and Sam.

'Sorry.' Sam was backing away. 'I didn't know...'

Roy shook his head, looked away. His head felt hot. He could only just control himself enough to step one pace back.

'Sam Bustard and Ben Shearer,' the girl from the bus said, bouncing the ball twice, then catching it on the top of her left foot.

Neither boy replied. Roy slumped on the low wall, feeling exhausted, and watched her, taking deep breaths. She pulled her hair up and tied it at the back, her eyes large and aggressive now.

'So, I take it from your third-rate banter that you're Tynecaster United fans now?' she asked Sam and Ben.

Still no reply.

The girl was flicking the ball from her right foot to her left. Slow controlled keepie-uppies.

Ben was still filming.

'I can tell you for a fact, Roy Race,' the girl said, still keeping the ball up, 'that Ben and Sam were Melchester Rovers fans until three years ago and that I know that because they *both* went to my high school and they *both* had Melchester Rovers scarves and they *both* used to go on about Melchester all the time.'

The girl increased the height of the ball, foot to foot, then let it rest on the back of her neck, where she held it still. Roy wondered how she knew his name. He had no idea what hers was. And how did she know about his dad being in a wheelchair?

'What happened, boys?' the girl asked, as the ball fell back to her feet, left then right and again.

Still nothing from Sam and Ben. They should have gone by now, but a small crowd had gathered around them and Ben was still filming the girl's skilful display. Voices calling out. Claps for when the girl lofted the ball and caught it on her foot, her head or her knee.

'You two,' the girl raised her voice, as she lifted the ball high, span on her heel and pushed it upwards with her left shoulder then her right, then caught it on her right knee, holding it there, 'are the worst kind of *glory* hunters I have ever met. As soon as Sewage United fade away, you'll move onto another team, because all you care about is not having someone coming up to you and doing what you've just done to Roy. When you do it you feel like you're better than him because you support a better team. You feel stronger. But in fact, you're weak.

'Roy Race, here, has supported Rovers as they've been relegated year after year and, even though he probably dreads seeing Tynecaster fans going on and on, he still supports Rovers which makes him – not you – the strong one. He's the real football fan.'

The girl flicked the ball up with the back of her heel. It came over her head, knocked the phone clean out of Ben's hands and sent it spinning into a bush. The girl caught the rebounding ball on her thigh.

Applause from the crowd. Fifty plus people round them now.

One voice calling out: 'You tell them, Ffion.'

Ben and Sam were just standing there, looking at each other, speechless.

And Roy Race knew her name now. Ffion.

THE ROW WITH Ben and Sam had actually
been good for Roy. It had taken his mind
off the final that evening – and the fact that
Johnny Dexter was coming to watch.

Back home, after college, Roy prepared
his kitbag, cracking his boots together in the
back yard to get rid of the dried mud and grass
coiled round the studs. He checked the rest
of his kit: shin pads, tape, top, shorts, socks.
Everything had to be clean and sorted. He
also packed a large bottle of salted squash,
two bananas and a double-thick slice of his
mum's homemade carrot cake.

Roy had his tea early when his mum got in at four-thirty. Beans on toast. Large. The perfect pre-match meal. Mum was at home all evening. No work for once: she always made sure she didn't work when Roy had a match.

Two and a half hours of pre-match nerves. Roy's chest felt like it had been over-pumped with air. His breathing was shallow. Jolts of electricity rippling through his shoulders and down his arms. But this was normal. Roy was used to it. He breathed in and out. He was on top of his nerves, keeping them down, keeping them controlled, so that he could harness them during the game.

Roy was ready. For the Moor Cup final. And to be looked over by Melchester Rovers.

He checked his kitbag one more time.

Then, while she was sorting out Dad's medication, Roy's mum's phone rang.

Roy picked it up, saw it was work and answered it, not wanting Mum to miss the call. A voice asked for Mrs Race.

'Mum?' Roy called.

Roy sat at the bottom of the stairs and watched his mum come quickly to the phone.

'It's work,' he told her.

'Hello?' Mum said.

Roy saw his mum looking at him as she listened to the voice on the phone, nodding. Next he saw her put her hand to her mouth and breathe out loudly. Roy tried to work out what the problem might be. He watched his mum mute the phone and open her mouth to speak to him.

And he guessed. He knew what this was about.

'It's the care home,' Mum said.

Roy swallowed.

'They're asking me to cover. They're short tonight. Just for an hour or two. What time's your game? Is Dexter still coming?'

'He is. Kick off at seven,' Roy replied, all the nervous energy that he'd been keeping just right draining out of him.

Mum's face was pale. She looked tired. Really tired. Roy could see she was torn. That she couldn't think what to say. She had a choice: let down work or let down her son.

Roy wanted to tell her to stay at home and rest. But he knew that, when extra shifts were offered, his mum had to go. If she didn't, someone else would be allocated the work and his mum might not get offered the hours again so easily.

And they needed the money. They always needed money. Since Dad was ill. That's why she was working three jobs.

'Go to work, Mum,' Roy said. 'I'll look after Dad. My knee's playing up anyway. I shouldn't play.'

'Liar,' Mum whispered.

Roy could see that Mum was close to tears: he had to make this easier for her. She had no choice, really.

'Melchester scout the local Under-18s all the time,' Roy said next, as convincingly as he could. 'I'll have another chance in a week or two.'

'Really?' Some colour had returned to Mum's face.

'Really,' Roy lied again. 'And, as it's the final today, I'll only be on the bench anyway. Yunis says I'm too young for a whole game, not strong enough for the Under-18s yet.'

'I'll be home by eight?' Mum suggested.

'Deal,' Roy grinned.

'If you're sure?' Mum looked at Roy. Roy looked back, staring into her eyes, willing her to believe him and not feel bad.

'Okay,' Mum said. She tapped her phone. 'I can be there in fifteen minutes,' she said. Then she grabbed her bag, checked her face and hair in the mirror, kissed Roy's dad and she was off.

'I'll definitely be back at eight,' she shouted over her shoulder. 'Be ready.'

'I will,' Roy said, standing in the doorway,

waving his mum off as she rushed down the street. He sat at the foot of the stairs again, screwing his eyes tight for a few seconds. Then he started to text Yunis, choosing his words carefully.

Mum was back at twenty to eight.

'Go,' she gasped, the key still in the door.

Roy snatched his bag and ran up his street. Turning at the top of the long terraced road he could hear the noises of park football. Shouts. Barking. A long whistle.

'Half time,' he said to himself. He wasn't too late.

Sprinting now, he crossed the road into the car park on the edge of the Moor, but was forced to change direction suddenly to avoid a black Range Rover that almost reversed into him. Roy stopped for a second, frightened by the near miss. Gazing around he saw Fred and his dog were walking behind the goal, the dog sniffing the netting. He jogged in the old man's direction, slowing as he came close to Fred and saw the Grimroyd players had slumped onto the floor around Yunis. Archie, the team's keeper, looked over at Roy and shrugged.

Not a good sign.

'Two-nil,' Fred informed Roy.

'Thanks, Fred.' Roy was gutted.

'He's gone,' Fred said next.

Roy wondered for a moment who Fred was talking about.

'What?'

'The so called "Hard Man",' Fred explained. 'He was the one who nearly ran you over.'

Roy closed his eyes. Dexter had gone. Being scouted: he'd blown it.

'I put a word in for you, son,' Fred said. 'With Dexter.'

Roy barely heard the old man. He could only hear what he'd said to his mum earlier.

Melchester scout the local Under-18s all the time. I'll get another chance in a week or two.

It wasn't true. That might have been his only chance. He was up against all the other sixteen-year-old boys in the country that wanted to be professional footballers.

Then Roy remembered the game. This game. The team he was part of. He shook his head. What was the matter with him, thinking about himself? There was a final to play.

'Thanks Fred,' Roy said. Then he jogged towards Yunis. To apologise.

* * *

Yunis put Roy on for the last half an hour. Some of the Grimroyd players were cramping already in the evening heat. The team needed fresh legs. And they were still 2-0 down.

Siddall – the other finalists – were playing defensively now, killing the game, protecting their lead. Every pass, every cut or thrust from Grimroyd just hit that wall. It was desperate. With twenty minutes to go it was still 2-0 to Siddall.

It looked hopeless. Even Vinny Samson was quiet, like he had accepted defeat, and just wanted it over.

Roy noticed his sister, standing watching. She must have come up after him. Rocky looked pale to Roy. He had always loved it when she came to watch him play football. He loved it that she was proud of him but he didn't quite feel that was the case after their chat earlier. Roy had to force himself to concentrate on the game and not feel bad that he was letting his sister down. He'd worry about her later. He was pleased to see Fred and Rover had gone over to talk to her.

'Set pieces,' Yunis shouted from the touchline. 'We need corners, free kicks. It's the only way. And get the ball on the wings. We need to go wide.'

Roy caught his coach's eye and put his thumb up, then he stood with his back to goal calling for the ball. He could win free kicks. Not by cheating or diving. Just by attacking so directly that the Siddall defence would be forced to foul him. Either that or he'd be through on goal.

Roy went at Siddall hard. He'd take on one or two defenders. Even three. Very quickly his tactic began to work, with the Siddall defence dropping deeper and his team mates taking inspiration from him, picking up their games, casting off their air of a defeated team.

But – even though Roy's first three attempts to attack directly ended fruitless – it was clear that, slowly but surely, something started to shift. The minds of the Siddall players were stuttering with nerves and doubt and fear.

Roy could smell it. There was hope for Grimroyd.

Spurred on, Roy turned to attack the penalty area again. A defender stuck his leg out to chop him down. But Roy skipped over the tackle and – one on one with the keeper – hit the ball hard.

GOAL!

It was in. 2-1. He'd scored his first goal.

A shout from the other players as Roy ran into the back of the goal to retrieve the ball. Brendan and Dave came to clap him on the back. Then Vinny grabbed the ball.

'Keep doing what you're doing, Racey,' Roy's captain said. 'We've got a chance now.'

And Roy wondered. Did they have a chance? Could they level the final? Even win it?

18

THE NEXT TIME Grimroyd attacked was down the wing. Vinny came crashing forward and managed to win a corner. But it was a poor corner that passed over all the players' heads and went dead.

Then a further attack, a pass from Kerrigan into Roy's feet. Roy tried to turn. Another foul.

Grimroyd's free kick hit the wall and Siddall counter-attacked up the field.

Time was running out. Just five minutes left.

Still 2-1 to Siddall.

Another Grimroyd attack: another foul. Roy down again. It seemed to Roy that Siddall were panicking now, not sure how to deal with Roy's frenzied one-on-one attacking. The intense game. The stifling heat. The fact this was a final. Every player was shattered, some of them cramping. Two Grimroyd players were helped off the pitch, meaning they were now down to nine men.

Roy paced the edge of the penalty area, waiting for Vinny to take the free kick.

They had to score. They were running out of players now, as well as time.

But now Vinny couldn't take the free kick. He'd taken a foul and was wincing with pain. Vinny was helped off and with no substitute to replace him or the others, Grimroyd were down to eight and without a captain. The Grimroyd keeper, Archie Achebe, came up to hammer the ball into the penalty area.

'This is madness,' Roy said to himself as he and the remaining players packed the penalty area. But there was no point in protecting their own goal: that made perfect sense to Roy. They had to risk everything to score a goal. If they conceded another it didn't matter.

The keeper's free kick was a beauty, soaring over the Siddall wall and the entire defence, who were confused as it dipped into the box, just yards ahead of Roy, who was running in on goal, bullying his way through the defence, forcing his forehead down on the ball as it hammered off the hard ground and bounced through the Siddall keeper's arms and into the roof of the net.

GOAL!

2-2.

The gamble had paid off.

But all the hard work had come at a price,

because now another Grimroyd player was down crying out in agony. As he was being treated by Yunis, Roy looked over to Rocky. There was a girl standing close to her. A bit taller than Rocky, with long red hair and big green eyes.

Ffion.

What was *she* doing here? Was it a coincidence? He wondered if she had talked to Rocky. Roy took a sudden breath. He had worked something out.

Rocky could talk to Ffion.

That was it.

Simple.

Surely, if anyone knew what opportunities there were for girls football in Melchester it had to be Ffion.

Roy had his answer to Rocky's problem.

His injured teammate was on his feet now. But putting his arm around Yunis, he was out of the game. Another man down. Meaning Grimroyd were down to seven players now.

Roy had to get his mind together. On the game. Not on Ffion and Rocky. He could think about that after the final whistle. Otherwise they might as well be down to six.

Seven would have no chance against eleven in extra time. There was time maybe for one more attack.

This was it.

All or nothing.

Roy demanded the ball and took it, working his way down the left, clipping it off the legs of one of two defenders blocking him. He'd won a corner. Now he looked at the referee, who was checking his watch. Would he blow the final whistle before Grimroyd had a chance to take it?

No. He signalled the corner. And Roy immediately heard a shout from behind him.

It was Archie, the Grimroyd keeper, storming forward to take the corner. Roy ran to fetch the ball and tossed it to him.

'Get into the box,' Archie shouted at Roy. 'This is it.'

Once Roy was in position, he watched as Archie took two steps back, then step up, ready to fire the ball into the area. At the same time – working on instinct – Roy backed out of the penalty area, confusing his markers, who had been expecting him to run back in to head the ball, like last time when he'd punished them with a header.

One chance.

Roy jogged over towards the corner flag, pretending he was going to receive the ball short. Then he changed direction, accelerated into the box as the ball came over, skimming off a head, dropping and bouncing high off the hard pitch.

Roy pushed on.

Found space.

And here it was, the ball, coming too high. It hit his chest, then dropped onto his left foot, as a defender came at him. And, in that moment, Roy remembered Ffion and her footwork at college earlier that day. He moved the ball onto his right foot, then flipped it up, over the defender, dodged round him and with his left foot, volleyed the ball past the stunned Siddall keeper.

GOAL!

3-2.

An extraordinary goal.

Seconds later, a long whistle.

And it was over.

Grimroyd Under-18s had won the Moor Cup for the first time in their history. Roy Race had scored a second half hat-trick. But before he could take it all in, Roy was mobbed by his teammates. One after the other jumping on top of him. A hand came down to him to help him out of the pile.

Vinny's.

'That,' his captain said, 'was a performance. Respect, Roy. Respect.'

Roy grinned. He'd never thought he'd hear Vinny say that.

But – even though he was happy, really happy – in the back of his mind, he wondered if he had blown his chance of playing for Melchester Rovers for good.

AFTER THE CONGRATULATIONS of his teammates
– and after he had shaken the hand of every
player on the opposition team – Roy glanced
over to check his sister was still behind the
goal.

She was.

Roy jogged over to her.

'Happy?' she asked.

'Yeah,' Roy grinned. 'Scored a hat-trick.
Why wouldn't I be?'

'Because… Fred told me about the scout,'
Rocky said.

Roy shrugged. 'Can't do anything about

163

that now,' he muttered. Then he gazed over to see Ffion still standing at the other side of the pitch.

'I'm sorry,' Rocky said. 'About that.'

Roy smiled. 'Don't worry about me. Listen, I want you to meet someone.'

'Who?'

'Just follow me.'

Roy and Rocky walked across the pitch towards Ffion, who had her head on one side, studying the two of them as they approached. Roy realised that, until today, he'd had no idea what he was going to say to Ffion when he got the chance.

But now he did.

Twenty metres. Ten metres. Face to face.

'Hi,' Roy said, glad his voice hadn't gone all weird and high-pitched. 'This is my sister, Rocky.'

'Hi, Rocky.' Ffion smiled. 'And Roy.'

Roy felt himself blush. There was a silence. A long one. Roy could see Rocky looking at him thinking, why is he being so weird? Why is he introducing us?'

'Rocky wants your advice,' Roy said.

'Sure,' Ffion smiled.

'About women's football.'

'*Women's* football?' Ffion raised an eyebrow.

Roy felt a slight panic around his throat. He had a feeling this girl who liked to mock boys at college was about to do a job on him.

'Her teachers,' he coughed, 'and... er... other people won't help her find a team to play for. She needs advice.'

'Why don't you give her advice?' Ffion smiled again.

Roy coughed. 'I er... I don't know what to tell her.'

'You don't know about football?' Ffion asked.

'Yeah, I know loads. Did you just see...'

'I saw you. Well done, by the way,' Ffion said, 'but we're not talking about you; we're talking about your sister.'

Roy heard Rocky snigger. She was enjoying this.

'Three questions,' Ffion said.

'Okay,' Roy agreed, dreading what was coming next.

'You think know about football, right?'

'Yeah.'

'But you only know about men's football, right?'

'Well, I've watched England women on TV.'

'But that's all? So, can you help your sister or not?'

'I suppose not,' Roy shifted his weight from one foot to the other.

'So you don't know about football? You only know about men's football.'

Roy paused. Then felt himself laughing. He saw the two girls looking at him. 'Yeah,' he admitted. 'I suppose you're right.'

'I'm part of a team,' Ffion said, turning to face Rocky. 'We love to get new players. Maybe you'd like to come down and see us tomorrow?'

Rocky nodded enthusiastically. 'Please.'

SUNDAY CAME. THE day scouted players were supposed to go to the trials at Mel Park. The trials Roy wasn't invited to.

Instead of trying out for his boyhood football team, Roy was with Dad, giving him a cup of tea, helping him lift it to his mouth, talking about winning the Moor Cup and his hat-trick.

He admitted to Dad that he'd missed out on being scouted for today's Melchester trial. He knew his dad would want to know and wouldn't accept being lied to.

'I'll get another chance, Dad,' Roy said

firmly. 'You know I will.'

Danny Race tried to smile.

Roy went on talking to his dad, speaking for both of them.

As he chattered on, Roy heard his dad make a noise. Something deep in his throat. Two muffled attempts at words.

'What's up, Dad? Do you need the toilet?'

Dad shook his head.

'Food? Drink? Something? What?'

Dad shook his head again. He looked angry, frustrated.

Then two noises. Clear noises. Words.

'Go. Now,' Roy's dad repeated.

Roy stared into his dad's eyes. 'Did I hear you right?' he asked.

Dad nodded, tried to smile, his eyelids drooping.

'Go now?'

A weak nod.

'To the trial?'

Dad nodded again.

'Just show up?' Roy asked. 'Walk in there? That's what you mean?'

Dad nodded.

Roy put his hand on his dad's right hand. For a second their eyes locked: they understood each other perfectly.

'Mum. I'm off out for a bit,' Roy shouted.

'Okay. But I need you back at six for your dad. Okay?'

'Okay, Mum.'

Out of the door, Roy Race was running. Down the hill this time. Down his street. To the bottom, then left. Along the main road, Mel Park in view.

He ran at medium pace. Warming up. So that if he dared do it, if he dared to crash the trial, he'd be ready right off.

He slowed when he reached the stadium.

Mel Park. The huge iron gates were shut and forbidding. He could hear voices. An adult barking orders. The thud of balls being hit.

How would he get in?

Roy jogged around the perimeter of the stadium. To the wire fence. The old familiar gap. Inside, he could see lads wearing Melchester track suits. Other lads in training bibs. And Johnny Dexter himself, putting the players through drills.

Roy stood by the hole in the fence, breathed in, then out. This was it then. Time to dare. Time to make a chance for himself and – this time – to take it.

Team Sheet

Several people helped me write *Scouted*. Rob Power (West Ham United), my editor, who dealt with every cross and shot fired at him without raising a sweat. David Luxton (Leeds United), who marshalled my defence alongside his two colleagues, Rebecca Winfield (Sheffield Wednesday) and Nick Walters (Tottenham Hotspur). Simon Robinson (Nottingham Forest), Brendan Kerrigan (Crystal Palace) and David Brayley (Swansea City). A three-man middle-aged midfield that would play the ball to Roy's feet all day long, given the chance. My wife and daughter (Leeds United), who joined me (Leeds United) on the front line of getting this book to – we hope – hit the back of the net.

THE STORY CONTINUES!

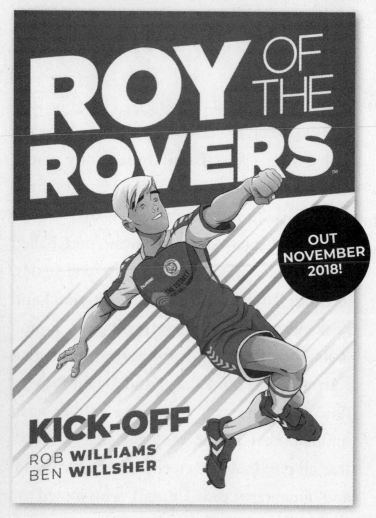

ROY OF THE ROVERS™

OUT NOVEMBER 2018!

KICK-OFF

ROB **WILLIAMS**
BEN **WILLSHER**

Will Roy impress the Rovers scouts? Does he have what it takes to become a pro? Find out in **ROY OF THE ROVERS: KICK-OFF**, the incredible new graphic novel out in November 2018!

For more **ROY OF THE ROVERS** find us online:

www.royoftheroversofficial.com